D0294204

THIS WALKER BOOK BELONGS TO:

_____

_____

_____

_____

EAST SUSSEX

V		INV No	
SHELF MARK			
COPY NO.			
BRN			
DATE	LOC	LOC	LOC	LOC	LOC	LOC

COUNTY LIBRARY

First published by Walker Books Ltd as
Big Bad Pig (1985), *Blow Me Down!* (1985),
Fee Fi Fo Fum (1985), *Help!* (1985), *Happy Worm* (1986),
Make a Face (1985) and *Tell Us a Story* (1986)

This edition published 1996

Text © 1985, 1986 Allan Ahlberg
Illustrations © 1985, 1986 Colin McNaughton

This book has been typeset in ITC Garamond Light.

Printed in Hong Kong

British Library Cataloguing in Publication Data
A catalogue record for this book is
available from the British Library.

ISBN 0-7445-4757-1

A RED NOSE COLLECTION

WHO STOLE THE PIE?

Allan Ahlberg + Colin McNaughton

WALKER BOOKS
AND SUBSIDIARIES
LONDON • BOSTON • SYDNEY

three little pigs and a big bad wolf

three big pigs and a big bad wolf

three little wolves and a big bad pig

three little bad pigs and a big wolf

three little pigs and
a big good wolf

TABLE + CHAIR

table + chair + boy + girl +

knife + fork + spoon + plate

+ sandwich + cake + jelly

+ drink + hat + cracker =

party

THE PIE

Who made the pie?

I did!

Who looked for the pie?

Who found the pie? Who ate the pie?

Who washed up?

CAT + FISH

pig + dinner = big pig

cow + grass = milk

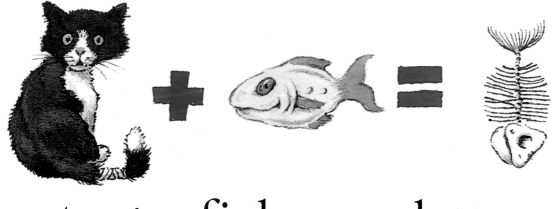

cat + fish = bones

BLOW ME DOWN!

"Blow me down!" says Burglar Bert. "Someone's pinched my football shirt."

"Blow me down!" says Burglar Paul. "Someone's pinched my bat and ball."

A catastrophe!

"Blow me down!" says Burglar Pat. "Someone's pinched my pussy cat."

"Blow me down!" says Burglar Jake. "Someone's pinched my birthday cake."

Crumbs!

Miaow!

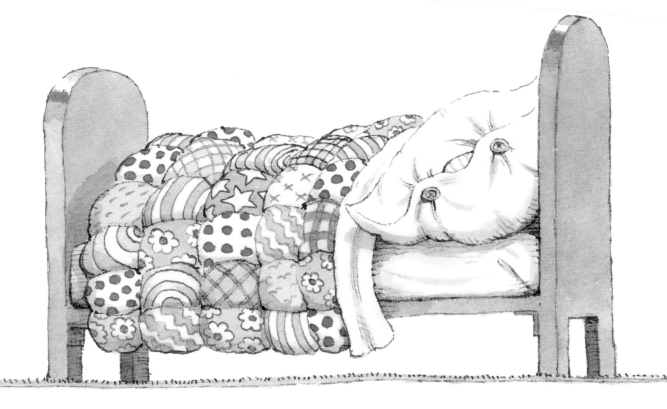

"Blow me down!"
says Burglar Freddy.
"Someone's pinched
my bedtime teddy."

MAKE A CASTLE

bucket   spade   flag   sand

make a castle

spade

flag

bucket

sand

drum   trumpet   boots   dog

make a noise

bread

bananas

jam

cheese

fish

grapes

sausages

beans

make a ...

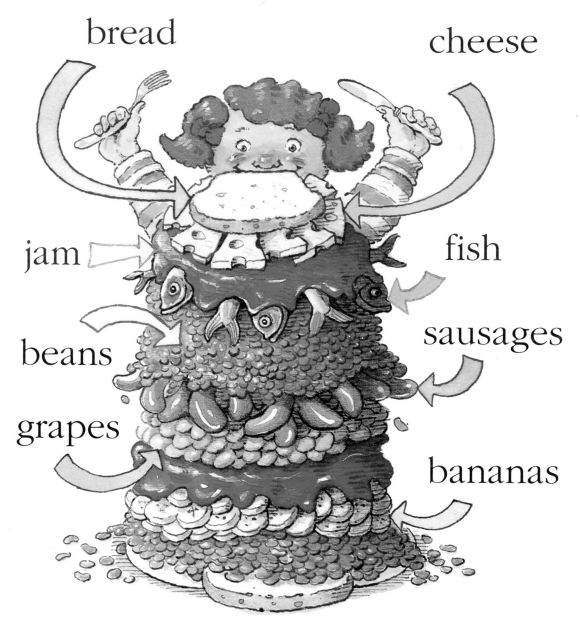

bread   cheese

jam   fish

beans   sausages

grapes   bananas

sandwich

The Pig

Two little boys climbed up to bed.

"Tell us a story, Dad,"
they said.

"Right!" said Dad.
"There was once a pig
who ate too much
and got so big
he couldn't sit down,
he couldn't bend…

Right!

So he ate standing up and got bigger –
The End!"

The Cat

"That story's no good, Dad," the little boys said. "Tell us a better one instead."

"Right!" said Dad. "There was once a cat who ate too much and got so fat he split his fur which he had to mend

Right!

with a sewing machine and a zip –
The End!"

The Horse

"That story's
too mad, Dad,"

the little
boys said.

"Tell us another
one instead."

"Right!" said Dad. "There was once a horse who ate too much and died, of course – The End."

The Cow

"That story's too sad, Dad,"
the little boys said.
"Tell us a happier one instead."

Right…

"Right… " said Dad.

"There was once a cow

who ate so much that even now

she fills two fields

and blocks a road,

and when they milk her
she has to be towed!

She wins gold cups
and medals too,
for the creamiest milk
and the *loudest* moo!"

Moo!

"Now that's the end,"
said Dad. "No more."
And he shut his eyes
and began to snore.

Then the two little boys climbed out of bed
and crept downstairs…

to their Mum instead.

The End

the end

MORE WALKER PAPERBACKS
For You to Enjoy

Also by Colin McNaughton

PUT ON A SHOW
written by Allan Ahlberg

You'll find creatures of all shapes and sizes –
from worms to monsters, from frogs to dogs –
in this madcap menagerie of single words and phrases,
simple sentences and memorable rhymes from
the popular Red Nose Reader series.

"The learning to read process
has never been more enjoyable."
Books For Your Children

0-7445-4756-3 £5.99

**HAVE YOU SEEN WHO'S JUST
MOVED IN NEXT DOOR TO US?**
Winner of the Kurt Maschler Award

King Kong, Mister Thing, ghouls, ghosties, aliens…
Meet the inhabitants of the weirdest street you could ever imagine!

"Highly entertaining… A book which can be re-read countless times
by a wide age-range." *Books For Your Children*

0-7445-3043-1 £4.99

WHO'S THAT BANGING ON THE CEILING?
"Inventive, wackily illustrated … it builds to a satisfyingly outrageous climax
in which King Kong is revealed in fold-out glory."
The Independent on Sunday

0-7445-3165-9 £4.99

Walker Paperbacks are available from most booksellers, or by post from B.B.C.S., P.O. Box 941, Hull, North Humberside HU1 3YQ

24 hour telephone credit card line 01482 224626

To order, send: Title, author, ISBN number and price for each book ordered, your full name and address,
cheque or postal order payable to BBCS for the total amount and allow the following for postage and packing:
UK and BFPO: £1.00 for the first book, and 50p for each additional book to a maximum of £3.50.
Overseas and Eire: £2.00 for the first book, £1.00 for the second and 50p for each additional book.

Prices and availability are subject to change without notice.